Rabbit Island

Story by Jörg Steiner
Illustrated by Jörg Müller

Translated by Anthea Bell

Hutchinson of London

Hutchinson & Co (Publishers) Ltd
3 Fitzroy Square, London W1P 6JD

Die Kanincheninsel first published by
Verlag Sauerländer AG, Aarau 1977
This translation first published by
Hutchinson & Co (Publishers) Ltd 1978
© Verlag Sauerländer AG 1977
Translation © Hutchinson & Co (Publishers) Ltd 1978
ISBN 0 09 132790 3
Printed in Switzerland

Factories where they make chocolate are chocolate factories. Factories where they make guns are gun factories.

But the factory in this book is a rabbit factory. It has no chimney, and it is not a very noisy place.

Instead of having machines, like other factories, the rabbit factory has conveyor belts running through it, carrying little cubes of rabbit food.

Hundreds of rabbits sit behind the conveyor belts in little cages, eating the cubes of rabbit food because they have nothing else to do. So they soon get fat. When they are fat enough they will be killed, but they don't know that. And they do not know if it is summer or winter, or day or night, because there are no windows in the factory, only soft artificial lighting.

One day a lorry stopped outside the factory, just as it did every day, and men opened the back of the lorry and carried some crates into the room full of conveyor belts.

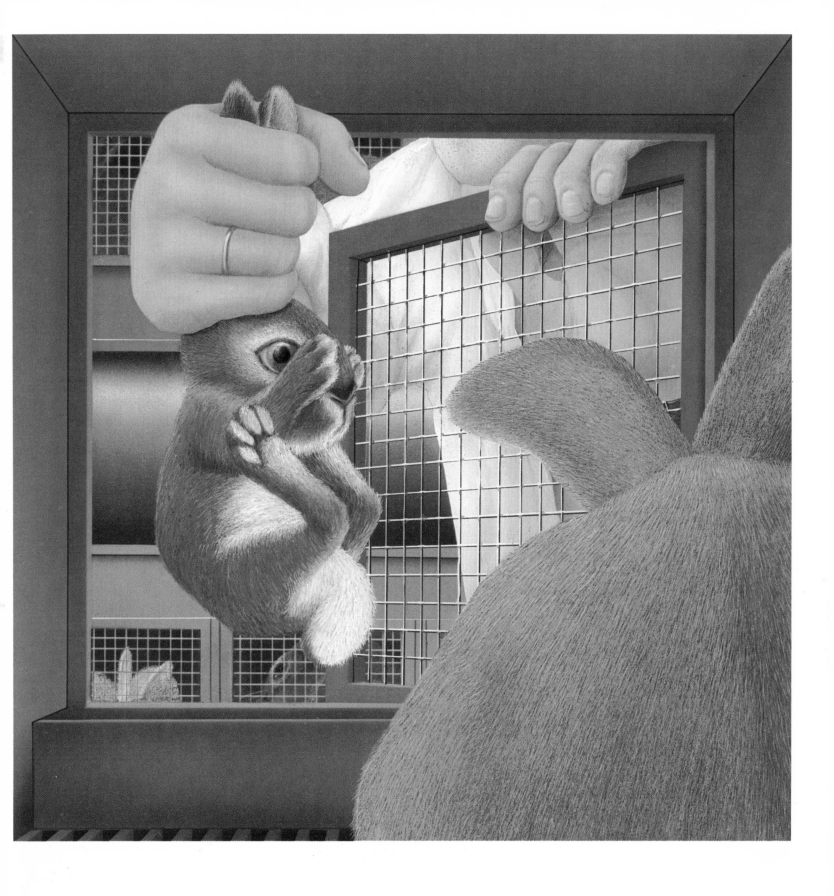

A big grey rabbit, who had been living in the factory for a long time, watched the men open the crates.

'Dear me, why are you trembling like that?' he asked a little brown rabbit who was just being lifted out of the first crate.

Little Brown huddled in the furthest corner of the cage.

'If you want to know anything, just ask me,' said Big Grey. 'I've been here a long time . . . yes, a very long time!'

'I'm scared,' whispered Little Brown. 'I'm so scared!'

'Oh, there's no need to be scared,' said Big Grey. 'We're very comfortable here. The men bring in crates of little thin rabbits, and then they fill up the crates with big fat rabbits and take them away, and that's the way the world goes round.'

'What happens to the big rabbits who get taken away?' asked Little Brown.

'Well, we don't know for sure,' said Big Grey, 'because none of them ever comes back. Myself, I think they go to an even better place. I've heard that there are huge white rabbits there.'

'As big as you?' asked Little Brown.

'Much bigger!' said Big Grey. 'Bigger than you can possibly imagine. The White Guardian Rabbits watch over all the others. They look after good rabbits, but they skin bad rabbits. If you're a good rabbit you live there happily ever after.'

Little Brown thought of the farm where he used to live until the men came in the lorry to take him away.

'I wonder if there are any carrots there?' he asked. 'I wonder if the sun shines in the daytime and the moon shines at night?'

Big Grey blinked. He had been in the factory so long that he had forgotten what carrots were like. However, he didn't want Little Brown to know that. 'Carrots, sun, moon . . .' he said, wrinkling up his nose. 'Oh, yes, they're all there.'

'Then the Land of the White Guardian Rabbits is just like my farmyard!' said Little Brown. 'And we'll be able to look for our own food! Do you remember grass and clover, and leaves and roots and bark?'

'Of course,' said Big Grey, untruthfully.

'I expect there are trees,' said Little Brown. 'And nice soft ground for digging rabbit holes.'

'I dare say,' said Big Grey, who had forgotten all about trees and nice soft ground.

'I was just thinking,' said Little Brown, 'we could go and find that lovely place ourselves. We needn't wait for the men to come and take us in a crate.'

'Not a bad idea,' said Big Grey, looking cautiously round. 'As a matter of fact, I've thought up a plan for getting out of here already. But then I'm big and strong, so the men are sure to come for me soon anyway.'

'What about me?' asked Little Brown. 'What shall I do, left without a friend?'

'Well, all right,' said Big Grey. 'Let's try my plan!'

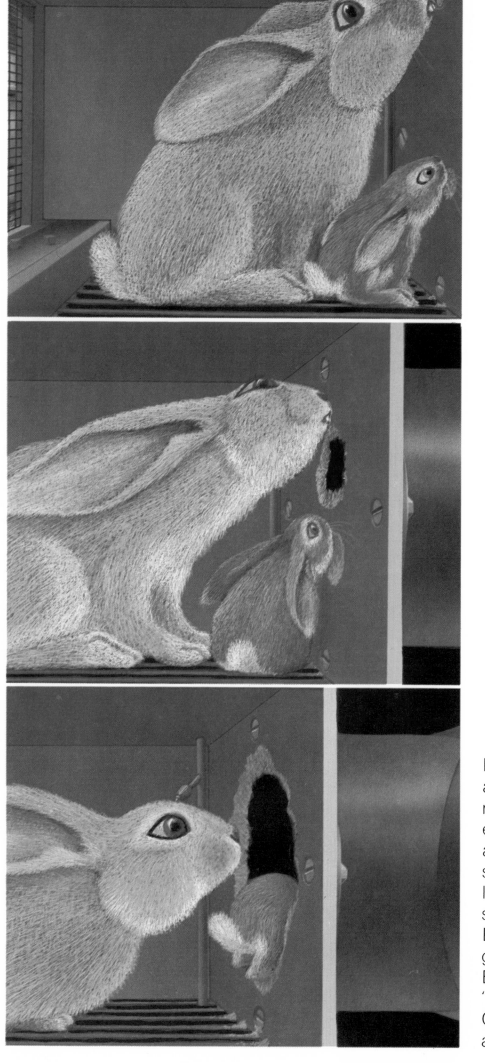

In actual fact, the idea of running away had never entered Big Grey's mind before. He had forgotten all he ever knew about things like flowers and rain and clouds and snow outside the factory, because he had lived there so long. But now he started gnawing away at his cage. Little Brown helped. When they had gnawed a big enough hole Little Brown slipped through.

'I hope I don't get stuck!' said Big Grey, as Little Brown scampered on ahead.

They scuttled along the ventilation shaft till they came to a round opening in the outside wall.

'We've done it, Big Grey!' whispered Little Brown. 'We're free!'

The two rabbits sat there for a long time, sniffing the air.

It was a warm summer night, and there was a cricket chirping nearby.

'Funny sort of smell,' whispered Big Grey at last.

'That's the smell of hay,' said Little Brown.

'Exactly!' said Big Grey, though he had forgotten what hay was, too.

They hopped happily through the grass, which was wet with dew. When Big Grey saw the way Little Brown pricked up his ears he did the same. Soon they came to a stream.

'Oh, look!' said Big Grey. 'Food will come along on that conveyor belt, just like it did at home!'

'I don't think that's a conveyor belt,' said Little Brown. 'I think it's a stream of water.'

'But it flows along, with a kind of rushing sound,' said Big Grey.

'Water flows too,' said Little Brown.

'Of course it does!' said Big Grey. 'Any fool knows that! How are we going to get across, that's the question?'

They hopped along beside the stream. Now and then Little Brown stopped to nibble at a leaf.

Then Big Grey sat up and looked around him.

'There's another stream over there,' he said. 'Only it's much wider, and it seems to be standing still.'

'That's not a stream,' said Little Brown. 'It's a road. I'm scared of roads.'

Big Grey did not see any reason to be scared of a road. 'I'll go first,' he said, and the two rabbits scampered across the road, Big Grey in front and Little Brown behind him.

On the other side of the road the ground was soft and sandy. The rabbits heard another rushing sound, but it was different from the sound of the stream, dryer and sharper. It was the wind rustling in the reeds.

'I'm terribly tired,' said Little Brown, hopping along behind Big Grey. 'Don't you think we ought to stop for a rest?'

Big Grey's paws were hurting him, too, but he said, looking round, 'Oh, I could keep going much longer! Still, I don't mind having a bit of a rest.'

So they both lay down in the dry reeds, and soon they fell asleep: Little Brown was tired because he was so small, and Big Grey was tired because he had forgotten how to run and jump, sitting in the rabbit factory all day long.

When they woke up it was broad daylight. The sun was blinding. Silvery fishes shot up out of the water.

'I'm hungry,' said Big Grey. 'Did you mention carrots?'

'Yes, I did,' said Little Brown, with his mouth full, 'but I don't know what a carrot field looks like. You might try a spot of dandelion. Or some of that clover.'

They hopped around, and Big Grey sniffed suspiciously at a leaf.

'I've never eaten this kind of food before,' he said sadly: another thing he had forgotten was how good dandelion and clover tasted. 'Anyway, I'm not really hungry.'

At that moment the reeds behind them parted, and a swan made for them, stretching out its long neck. Frightened to death, the two rabbits scampered off.

'That was one of the White Guardian Rabbits, coming to skin us because we ran away!' gasped Big Grey.

It was some time before they realized that the swan had gone away, back to its young. The two exhausted rabbits cowered in the shade of a tree.

'Well, it's gone now,' said Little Brown, who was still out of breath. 'Do you think it was really a White Guardian Rabbit?'

'What else could it be?' asked Big Grey.

'It didn't look like a rabbit,' said Little Brown. 'And it came over the water.'

'Oh, the White Guardian Rabbits can swim,' said Big Grey. 'They can swim and fly and all sorts of things!'

Little Brown thought this over. 'Well, don't let's argue,' he said at last. 'Whatever it was, we've got work to do. We must dig a hole and then we'll be safe inside it, away from the blinding sunlight.'

And he jumped up and started to dig. 'Come on, Big Grey!' he called. 'Come and help!'
But Big Grey dared not come out of the shade. 'My head aches!' he wailed. 'And the White Guardian Rabbits are after us, and I can't find any food, and I don't know how to dig holes. I want to go home! It was nicer there!'
'I didn't like it much myself,' said Little Brown. 'And we still don't know what happens to the big fat rabbits when they're taken away. They don't seem to be here do they?'
Big Grey huddled closer to the tree, and now and then a shudder ran right through him. Little Brown was alarmed. 'What's the matter, Big Grey?' he asked. 'Why are you so quiet?'
But Big Grey did not answer.
Little Brown made up his mind. 'Big Grey, I'll take you home if you like,' he said. 'I know the way now, and my hole will be waiting here for me when I come back.'
Big Grey still lay there like a dead rabbit, but he gradually stopped shuddering. 'Would you really take me home?' he asked at last.
'Of course!' said Little Brown. 'We're friends, aren't we?'
'I'll never forget what you've done for me,' promised Big Grey. 'Not as long as I live!'

The hot sun was shining down through the treetops, and not a breath of wind stirred the reeds. There was a man standing by the water, fishing. His dog lay beside him, twitching in his sleep.

When the fisherman saw the two rabbits, he whistled. 'Hey, you!' he said quietly to his dog. 'Look at you, lying there dreaming of hunting, while the fattest wild rabbits you ever saw hop by right in front of your nose.'

The man had never actually seen a wild rabbit. These two act like ordinary tame rabbits, he thought, except that tame rabbits belong to someone, they don't run about loose.

Gently, he put down his rod, crouched down and waited.

He almost caught Little Brown, who had not seen him. But Little Brown gave a tremendous wriggle and got away. The dog woke up, growling, and Big Grey and Little Brown ran for their lives. They ran and ran.

They were not trying to keep under cover any more, they just raced back the way they had come the night before. The dog chased them as far as the road and then stopped. He began to bark, his coat bristled — but he dared not cross the road.

The rabbits lay in the tall grass beside the stream, panting. They waited there till evening.

Big Grey was the first to speak. 'Are you still alive, Little Brown?' he asked.

'I think so,' said Little Brown.

'We'll soon be home now,' said Big Grey. 'Then we'll be all right! We ran away together and now we're going home together..'

Little Brown shook his head sadly. 'Big Grey, you know I can't go back with you,' he said.

'You could if you wanted to!' said Big Grey. 'Aren't you scared of those White Guardian Rabbits?'

'Yes, I am,' said Little Brown. 'And I'm scared of the road, and I'm scared of men and dogs trying to catch me.'

'You're very brave,' said Big Grey. 'And you know your way around better than me. I've forgotten too much.'

'I can see the factory lights over there,' said Little Brown. 'I'll go as far as the factory with you, and then we must say goodbye.' The two rabbits hopped along beside the hedges and over to the buildings with their soft artificial lighting.

But the closer they came, the less familiar the buildings looked. 'That's not our factory,' whispered Little Brown, at last.

'It looks very like it, though,' said Big Grey. He began trembling again. 'Maybe it's a factory for bigger animals?'

'Maybe,' agreed Little Brown. 'Don't worry, we'll find the way home for you.'

And at last they did.

Before moonrise, the two rabbits were slipping under the fence.

There was a smell of hay, and a cricket was chirping somewhere nearby.

'I can't stay long,' said Little Brown. 'I ought to start back at once.'

'I expect you're right,' whispered Big Grey. 'Don't forget me, back there in your hole! Whatever shall I do without you?'

'You'll find a new friend,' said Little Brown. 'I'm sure you will.'

'I'll never find another friend like you,' said Big Grey — but Little Brown did not hear him. He was already over by the fence again.

'Good luck, Little Brown!' called Big Grey. 'Good luck!'

5341

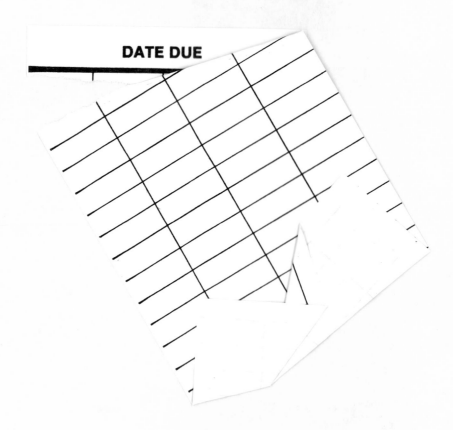